# Burro's Tortillas

## By Terri Fields
## Illustrated By Sherry Rogers

To two very *punny* and wonderful people Jack and Charlene Shaffer, with lots of love to Ashley Taylor Malkin, Spencer and Ethan Scher, Julia and Michael Baumel, and always to my muses, Jeff, Lori, Rick, and Mom—TF

To Mom, Dad, and my sister Diane, for their loving support in all I do—SR

Thanks to Elizabeth Wolanyk, Director of Education and Research at the American Farm Bureau Foundation for Agriculture for verifying the accuracy of the information in the "For Creative Minds" educational section.

Publisher's Cataloging-In-Publication Data

Fields, Terri, 1948-
Burro's tortillas / by Terri Fields ; illustrated by Sherry Rogers.

p. : col. ill. ; cm.

In this Southwestern retelling of a childhood favorite, Burro finds it difficult to get any help from his friends as he diligently works to turn corn into tortillas. "For Creative Minds" section includes a Spanish/English glossary and a simple recipe for making tortillas.

ISBN: 978-0-9768823-9-8 (hardcover)
ISBN: 978-1-934359-18-1 (pbk.)

1. Donkeys--Juvenile fiction.  2. Tortillas--Juvenile fiction.  3. Donkeys--Fiction.
4. Tortillas--Fiction.  5. Folklore.  I. Rogers, Sherry.  II. Title.

PZ8.1.F47918 Bu 2007
398.2/45 [E]          2006940902

Printed in China

Sylvan Dell Publishing
976 Houston Northcutt Blvd., Suite 3
Mt. Pleasant, SC 29464

Once upon a time, not so long ago, a little burro saw that the corn had grown very tall. And right away, he thought,

## TORTILLAS!

He called his friends. "Whinee aw ah aw. *Mis amigos—vengan aquí.*"

The bobcat, the coyote, and the jackrabbit came immediately.

"*Amigos*, look at all this wonderful corn!" said the burro. "Who will help me pick the corn so we can make *tortillas*?"

"*Yo no,*" said the bobcat. "I'm too cool a cat to pick corn."

"*Yo no,*" said the coyote. "I'm taking a coyo tea break."

"*Yo no,*" said the jackrabbit. "I've really got to hop along."

"Then I will pick the corn myself," the little burro said to himself.

And he did . . .

He picked so much white corn that he could hardly carry it home on his back.

When he got home, he gathered his friends again. "*Amigos*," he said. "I have picked the corn. Who will help me remove the kernels?"

"*Yo no*," said the bobcat. "Scratch me from that job."

"*Yo no*," said the coyote. "I'm doing trickier things."

"*Yo no*," said the jackrabbit. "I'm having a bad hare day."

"Then I will remove the kernels myself," said the burro.

And he did . . .

He took corn and removed all the kernels from the cobs.

Then he gathered up all the kernels, boiled them with lime, rinsed them off, and set them aside to dry.

The little burro looked at his hard work. He had done a lot, but there was still much to do before the corn became *tortillas*.

"Whinee aw ah aw," he called, "The corn is ready to be ground into flour. Who wants to use the grinding stone first?"

"*Yo no*," said the bobcat. "I'm too busy growling."

"*Yo no*," said the coyote. "I'm too busy howling."

"*Yo no*," said the jackrabbit. "I'm too busy being all ears."

The burro sighed, for he really was tired but he was also stubborn.

"Fine, then I will grind the corn myself."

And he did . . .

He stood over the *metate* and used the pestle to grind the corn.

When he finished, he called,

"*Amigos*, the corn is ground. Who will help me make *la masa*? It is not as much work as grinding. And if you want, you can growl or howl or listen while you do it."

"*Yo no*," yawned the bobcat. "I'm catching a little cat nap."

"*Yo no,*" yawned the coyote. "I'm already counting sheep."

"*Yo no*," yawned the jackrabbit. "Hare now, gone to *siesta*."

The very tired burro wanted to take a nap too . . .

. . . but he didn't.

He made small little balls of dough. This time, he didn't even call his friends when it was time to put each ball onto *la tortillera* to flatten it into a *tortilla* shape.

When he finished, the burro looked at the results of all his work and smiled. His mouth was watering. Very soon he could eat *tortillas muy deliciosas*. But first he had to get them onto the griddle before the dough dried out.

He called for his friends. "Whinee aw ah aw. *Amigos!* Your naps are over, and we are at the last step. Who will help me cook the *tortillas*?" His friends gathered round.

"*Yo no,*" said the bobcat, "I'm too purr-fect to cook."

"*Yo no,*" said the coyote. "It's not my territory."

"*Yo no,*" said the jackrabbit, "Even the idea is hare raising!"

"Then I will cook them myself," said the little burro.

And he did . . .

He put each flat circle on the
griddle, and turned it over and over until it
was fully cooked. Soon he had a big basket
filled with fresh *tortillas*. They looked
wonderful, and they smelled even better.

And when he turned around, the little burro didn't have to call the bobcat, the coyote, or the jackrabbit. They were already standing right there.

He looked at all of them. They only looked at the basket of freshly made *tortillas*. "Who will help me eat all these *tortillas?*" asked the burro.

"*Yo,*" said the bobcat. "I'm primed to pounce!"

"*Yo,*" said the coyote. "Their scent is super!"

"*Yo,*" said the jackrabbit. "Hare's looking at you, let's eat!"

As the little burro reached for the *tortillas* to share with his *amigos*, he paused, and he thought, and then he said: "You did not help me pick the corn. You did not help me shell the corn. You did not help me boil the corn with lime. You did not help me grind the corn. You did not help me make *la masa*. You did not help me make the tortillas . . . and do you know what? Thank you, but I do not think I need any help to eat them!"

And he **DIDN'T.**

# For Creative Minds

## Corn: from plant to table

People in the area that we now know as Mexico and Central America have been growing corn for over five thousand years! They actually created corn by breeding two unlike plants. Even today, corn is an important part of the diet and culture in this part of the world.

It used to be that people would only be able to eat the types of foods that grew close to where they lived or came from animals nearby. Now we can grow plants all over the world by planting seeds, using irrigation, or using greenhouses. Modern transportation like ships, trains, trucks, and airplanes helps us to get food from other parts of the world.

Sometimes we eat the seeds or the fruit of the plant just the way we grow them, (apples, strawberries, or carrots). Or we may only eat a part of the plant such as the stem (celery), leaves (lettuce), or the flower (broccoli). We may also prepare it before eating (corn-on-the-cob). Sometimes grain (such as corn) is ground (into flour or cornmeal) and used to make other types of food that we eat.

Can you match some of the ways we eat corn? How do you think the corn was prepared to make these foods?

1.   Tortillas     _____

2.   Popcorn     _____

3.   Corn-on-the-cob     _____

4.   Corn chips     _____

5.   Cornbread     _____

6.   Corn flake cereals     _____

7.   Corn fritters     _____

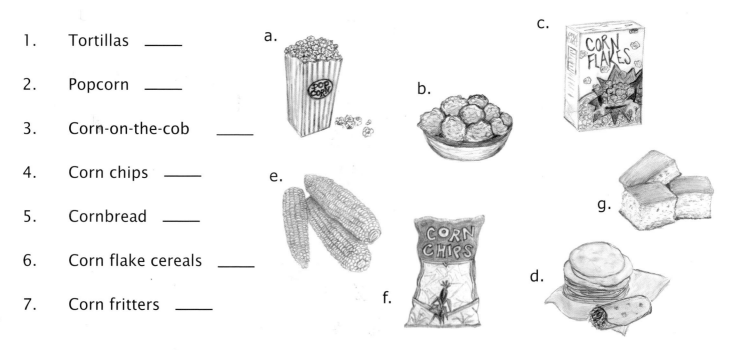

Answers: 1d; 2a; 3e; 4f; 5g; 6c; 7b

# *Spanish*/English vocabulary

Can you match the Spanish word to the English definition and the picture? Answers are upside down at the bottom of the page.

1.  *Tortillas*   \_\_\_\_

2.  *Mis amigos*  \_\_\_\_

3.  *Yo no*   \_\_\_\_

4.  *Metate*   \_\_\_\_

5.  *La masa*   \_\_\_\_

6.  *Siesta*   \_\_\_\_

7.  *Tortillera*  \_\_\_\_

a.  Dough

b.  Rest time during the heat of the day

c.  Not I

d.  A press to flatten the ball of dough

e.  A flatbread traditionally made out of corn but sometimes out of wheat

f.  Friends

g.  A stone used to grind corn using a pestle, a mortar

Answers: 1e; 2f; 3c; 4g; 5a; 6b; 7d

# Making *Tortillas*

The word *tortilla* comes from the Spanish word "*torta,*" which means "round cake." When the Spaniards came to Mexico in the sixteenth century, they found the Aztecs making and eating a most unusual food—corn. Sometimes the corn was made into the round cakes the Spaniards named *tortillas.* Today, some people still make *tortillas* from scratch, much the way the Mexican Indians once did and a lot like the way the little burro makes his *tortillas* in this book

You can make *tortillas* too. You can buy the special corn flour, called *maseca*, at a grocery or Mexican store. *Maseca* is made just as Burro did in the story, by cooking corn with a little lime (not the lime fruit, but a special lime that comes from burning limestone). It is then rinsed, dried and ground into the flour for us to use.

## What you will need to make 8 *tortillas:*

1 cup *maseca*
1 Tbs. corn or vegetable oil (optional)
¾ cup warm water
Mixing bowl and spoon or mixer
Slightly damp paper towels

Wax paper
Rolling pin
Cast iron skillet or griddle
Spatula

In a large bowl, mix together the *maseca,* the oil if using (this is not traditional but may help to hold the tortillas together while rolling) and the water. Mix together until the dough is smooth and forms a dough ball—about two or three minutes. The dough should be smooth but not too sticky.

Divide the dough into 8 little balls and cover with the slightly damp paper towels to keep them from drying out.

Cut off two square pieces of wax paper. Place one ball of dough at a time between the two sheets and use the rolling pin to roll into a circle (as best as you can).

With an adult's help, cook on a very hot, ungreased cast iron skillet or griddle. Use your spatula to flip the tortilla every 15 to 20 seconds until cooked (light brown). Wrap cooked tortillas in a small kitchen towel or cloth to keep warm and to prevent them from drying out.